LIFE IN THE MILITARY

LIFE IN THE
US COAST GUARD

by Cecilia Pinto McCarthy

BrightPoint Press

San Diego, CA

© 2021 BrightPoint Press
an imprint of ReferencePoint Press, Inc.
Printed in the United States

For more information, contact:
BrightPoint Press
PO Box 27779
San Diego, CA 92198
www.BrightPointPress.com

ALL RIGHTS RESERVED.

No part of this work covered by the copyright hereon may be reproduced or used in any form or by any means—graphic, electronic, or mechanical, including photocopying, recording, taping, web distribution, or information storage retrieval systems—without the written permission of the publisher.

LIBRARY OF CONGRESS CATALOGING-IN-PUBLICATION DATA

Names: McCarthy, Cecilia Pinto, author.
Title: Life in the US Coast Guard / by Cecilia Pinto McCarthy.
Description: San Diego : ReferencePoint Press, [2021] | Series: Life in the military | Includes bibliographical references and index. | Audience: Grades 10-12
Identifiers: LCCN 2020002436 (print) | LCCN 2020002437 (eBook) | ISBN 9781682829738 (hardcover) | ISBN 9781682829745 (eBook)
Subjects: LCSH: United States. Coast Guard. | United States. Coast Guard--Vocational guidance.
Classification: LCC VG53 .M378 2021 (print) | LCC VG53 (eBook) | DDC 363.28/60973--dc23
LC record available at https://lccn.loc.gov/2020002436
LC eBook record available at https://lccn.loc.gov/2020002437

CONTENTS

AT A GLANCE	4
INTRODUCTION	6
A DARING RESCUE	
CHAPTER ONE	12
HOW DO PEOPLE JOIN THE COAST GUARD?	
CHAPTER TWO	28
WHAT JOBS DOES THE COAST GUARD OFFER?	
CHAPTER THREE	46
WHAT IS A TYPICAL DAY LIKE IN THE COAST GUARD?	
CHAPTER FOUR	58
WHERE DO GUARDSMEN SERVE?	
Glossary	74
Source Notes	75
For Further Research	76
Index	78
Image Credits	79
About the Author	80

AT A GLANCE

- The US Coast Guard (USCG) is a branch of the US Armed Forces. It is also a federal law enforcement agency.

- Members of the USCG are called Guardsmen or Coasties. They protect and defend US waters and coastlines. They also patrol international waters. They make sure people follow laws at sea.

- More than 87,000 people serve in the USCG. Most are active duty. They work full-time. Others are in the US Coast Guard Reserve. They work part-time.

- Guardsmen perform rescues. They save people who are stranded at sea.

- Guardsmen also protect the environment. They help clean up oil spills.

- Coast Guard recruits must go through eight weeks of basic training. They must pass fitness and aptitude tests.

- Guardsmen have many career options. Some work at inland stations. Others work on large ships called cutters. The USCG has stations all over the United States.

- Guardsmen can receive specialized job training at "A" schools. These schools help them develop and strengthen certain skills.

INTRODUCTION

A DARING RESCUE

At 2:00 a.m. on September 8, 2019, an emergency call went out. The call came from a large cargo ship called the *Golden Ray*. The ship was carrying 4,000 cars. It was just off the coast of Brunswick, Georgia. At first, it had tilted. Then it rolled onto its left side. Onboard was a crew of twenty-four people.

The Golden Ray *cargo ship was 656 feet (200 m) long.*

The US Coast Guard (USCG) Air Station Savannah jumped into action. The Guardsmen began by rescuing the *Golden Ray*'s crew. A USCG helicopter

USCG boat and helicopter crews worked together to rescue the crew of the Golden Ray.

flew overhead. Guardsmen on the aircraft lowered a basket on a towline. One by one, the crew members climbed into the basket. The Guardsmen pulled them up to safety. Twenty crew members were rescued.

But four were still missing. To make matters worse, the *Golden Ray* was now on fire.

In the dark, the Guardsmen worked to find the missing crew members. They tapped on the outside of the ship. Three people inside the ship tapped back. The Guardsmen found the fourth person in another room. They cut a hole in the ship. The rescue took forty hours. But by the end, every crew member was saved.

WHAT IS THE COAST GUARD?

The USCG performs rescues at sea. It also has many other jobs. The USCG is a branch of the US Armed Forces. Men and women in the USCG are called Guardsmen. They are also commonly called Coasties. Coasties protect the United States in both peacetime and times of war.

The USCG is also a federal law enforcement agency. It enforces **maritime** laws. These are laws about what people can do at sea. The USCG protects marine environments too. Guardsmen oversee 100,000 miles (160,900 km) of US coastline and inland waterways. They also patrol in international waters.

Some Guardsmen patrol along the Hudson River in New York.

CHAPTER ONE

HOW DO PEOPLE JOIN THE COAST GUARD?

People join the USCG for many reasons. Some want to learn valuable skills. They are looking for a meaningful career. Captain Tom Walsh says, "I joined because it's not just a military branch for war. . . . You can do something every day that matters."[1]

The USCG does search-and-rescue exercises to train Guardsmen. Guardsmen are lowered from a helicopter.

Joining the USCG is a big commitment. Most people choose active-duty service. They serve full-time. They may be called to work at any time. The USCG has about 40,000 active-duty members.

REQUIREMENTS

There are basic requirements for applying to the USCG. An applicant must be a US citizen or a resident alien. A resident alien is a permanent US resident but not a citizen. Applicants must be between the ages of seventeen and thirty-one.

THE COAST GUARD'S MOTTO

The USCG's motto is *Semper Paratus*. This is a Latin phrase. It means "Always Ready." The motto describes the USCG. Guardsmen are always ready to act.

No one is sure how this phrase became the USCG's motto. The motto can be traced back to the early 1900s. In 1922, Captain Francis Saltus Van Boskerck wrote the USCG's official song. The song is called "Semper Paratus."

People who are thirty-two years old can join in special cases. People who are seventeen years old need parental permission. Applicants must have a high school diploma. Sometimes a General Education Diploma is accepted.

People who meet these requirements can interview with recruiters. Recruiters review the applicants' character. They look for people who are serious about joining the USCG. Recruiters give applicants more information. Applicants learn about jobs, pay, and benefits. They also learn about the training and length of service.

Applicants fill out many forms. They also must provide documents such as a birth certificate. They go through a background check.

APTITUDE TESTING

Next, applicants start the **enlistment** process. People who enlist are called recruits. They take the Armed Services Vocational **Aptitude** Battery (ASVAB) test. The ASVAB assesses verbal and math skills. It also measures science and technical skills. Technical skills include the ability to use certain tools. Recruits must score at least a forty to pass the test.

Guardsmen who want to change jobs or become officers may retake the ASVAB to try to get higher scores.

ASVAB scores show a person's strengths. They help match the person with a job. For example, one person may have high math and science scores. She might do well as an electrician. Another person may score high on the verbal test. He may be placed in a communication job.

BOOT CAMP

Another requirement is a medical exam. Doctors make sure recruits are in good health. Recruits who pass the ASVAB and this exam can move on. They take an oath to serve the United States. Most recruits agree to serve for eight years. The first four years are spent on active duty. The last four years are spent in the US Coast Guard Reserve. Reserve members serve part-time. They work one weekend a month and two weeks a year.

Company commanders yell instructions at recruits during boot camp. Their goal is to prepare recruits for high-stress situations.

The next step is basic training. This training is also called boot camp. It takes fifty-three days. It happens at a training center in Cape May, New Jersey.

Recruits learn to obey orders. The training is challenging. About 20 percent of recruits do not get through basic training. Petty Officer 2nd Class Reilly Burrus trains recruits. She explains, "We need to make sure that only the strong get through this."[2]

FORMING

The first few days of boot camp are called forming. Officers test recruits on their knowledge of the USCG. Recruits go through another medical exam. Then they must pass a physical fitness test. They must do as many sit-ups and push-ups as they can in one minute. They have to complete

COMPANY COMMANDERS

Recruits are part of groups called companies. All recruits are sorted into companies in the first week of boot camp. Each company can have up to 120 recruits. Company Commanders (CCs) lead the companies. They are strict. When one recruit makes a mistake, the entire company pays for it. Recruits have to do push-ups or run laps. CCs are tough. Their job is to turn recruits into confident, skilled Guardsmen.

a 1.5-mile (2.4-km) run. Men must finish the run in fourteen minutes. Women have seventeen minutes. Recruits who do not pass the fitness test get one more chance.

Next comes a swimming test. First, recruits jump off a platform into a pool.

The platform recruits must jump off of is 5 feet (2 m) high.

They must swim 328 feet (100 m) in five minutes or less. Then they must tread water for five minutes.

LEARNING NEW SKILLS

Boot camp includes hours of physical training. Recruits get up at 5:30 a.m. Then they work out. Workouts include running, sit-ups, push-ups, and swimming. Recruits practice skills such as treading water.

Recruits also take classes. They learn about the military justice system. They also study Coast Guard history and military customs.

Much of the recruits' education is hands-on. They learn how to tie knots and handle lines. They also learn how to steer boats and ships. After graduation, many Guardsmen will patrol waterways. Classes cover how to handle and fire weapons. Recruits are also trained to fight fires and perform first aid.

Recruits take a midterm exam after four weeks of boot camp. The exam tests their knowledge. Recruits must get a score of at least 80 percent.

Recruits can request where they would like to serve. But the USCG has the final say. Guardsmen are stationed wherever they are most needed. Recruits learn where they will be stationed at the end of the fifth week of boot camp. They may be assigned to work onshore. Or they may work on board a ship. There are many USCG bases around the country. Guardsmen may be stationed along a coast.

Recruits spend hours in class preparing for the written final exam.

FINAL EXAMS AND GRADUATION

Before they can graduate, recruits need to pass final exams. These are written and physical tests. The written exam covers everything recruits have learned in class. The physical exams are timed. Men must do thirty-eight sit-ups in one minute.

They also must do twenty-nine push-ups in a minute. Women must do thirty-two sit-ups in a minute. They have a minute to do fifteen push-ups.

THE US COAST GUARD RESERVE

Some people are part of the US Coast Guard Reserve. They are called reservists. They work part-time for the USCG. They go through boot camp. Then they return home. Many work or attend college full-time. Reservists train one weekend each month with their unit. They also devote two weeks a year to full-time duties. Some reservists are members of the USCG Auxiliary. They are volunteers. They teach boating safety classes to the public. They also do **vessel** safety checks and assist with other duties.

Recruits must again do a 1.5-mile (2.4-km) run. Men have to do this in twelve minutes and fifty-one seconds. Women have to do this in fifteen minutes and twenty-six seconds. Another part of the physical exam is a swim test. Recruits jump off a platform into a pool. Then they swim 328 feet (100 m).

Recruits who pass the final exams graduate. They go through a graduation ceremony. Family and friends attend the celebration. Recruits take five days off after the ceremony. Then it's time for their first assignment.

CHAPTER TWO

WHAT JOBS DOES THE COAST GUARD OFFER?

Guardsmen have a variety of jobs. They investigate boating accidents. They also inspect vessels. They seize drugs and arrest criminals. Some Guardsmen fly aircraft. They help with search-and-rescue (SAR) missions. They often save people who are stranded at sea.

Some Guardsmen train to become pilots. They learn how to land and take off from a USCG vessel.

Guardsmen get on-the-job training. At first, they try many jobs. They learn what they are good at. They discover which jobs they enjoy most. USCG job types fall into four groups. One group works with vessels and weapons. Another group works with machinery. Some people work with aircraft. And others help support the USCG.

VESSELS AND WEAPONS

Many Guardsmen work with vessels and weapons. The USCG has nearly 1,900 vessels. These vessels include cutters. Cutters are large ships. Each cutter is at least 65 feet (20 m) long. Vessels smaller than cutters are called boats.

Many jobs are available on vessels. Some Guardsmen become boatswain's mates (BMs). They learn many skills. They work on every type of vessel, from cutters

Some cutters are more than 200 feet (60 m) long.

to small tugboats. BMs may stand watch for security. They can operate cranes and load cargo. They also navigate boats on SAR missions. Sometimes they arrest criminals. BMs need to be physically strong. They also need to have good leadership skills.

Another important job is gunner's mate (GM). GMs handle weapons and explosives.

They also teach other Guardsmen how to use weapons. On a typical day, a GM cleans and repairs guns. Later, he may train other Guardsmen to shoot. GMs have good math and mechanical skills.

Other people work as Maritime Enforcement Specialists (MEs). They are police officers. They board vessels to do safety checks. They make sure vessels have safety equipment such as life vests. MEs patrol at sea. They search vessels for drugs. They can arrest drug smugglers. They also watch for people trying to enter the country illegally.

Some MEs may train or work with dogs. The dogs are trained to sniff out weapons or drugs.

MACHINERY

The USCG needs electricians and technicians. These people make sure machines work properly. Some Guardsmen become damage controlmen (DCs).

An electronics technician fixes a radar system on a USCG cutter. Radar systems have many parts.

They have many skills. They fix machines that stop working or are damaged. They are also trained to clean up chemical spills.

Guardsmen who have electrical skills can become electrician's mates (EMs). EMs need math and technical knowledge.

They install and maintain equipment. They also do repairs. Some EMs maintain power generators and motors. These devices help power vessels. EMs also work on communication and navigation equipment. Many EMs have advanced engineering and technology training.

Electronics technicians work on radios and televisions. They also maintain radar and navigation equipment. Radar is used to find objects. A device sends out sound waves. The waves bounce off an object such as a ship. The device measures how long it takes for the sound wave to return.

This gives information about the object's location and speed.

AIRPLANES AND HELICOPTERS

The USCG has about 200 aircraft. The aircraft move at fast speeds. Pilots can respond quickly during SAR missions.

USCG aircraft also patrol waterways. Guardsmen look for vessels that use illegal fishing nets. Fishing nets must be a certain size. They also must be made of certain materials. Large nets can capture animals such as sharks. This type of fishing is illegal.

Other guardsmen are avionics electrical technicians (AETs). They inspect and repair an aircraft's electrical equipment. Aviation maintenance technicians (AMTs) check parts such as the engines and wings. They ensure a plane's fuel and power systems are working.

USCG VESSELS

The USCG uses many types of vessels. Icebreakers can smash through ice. Guardsmen use these vessels in the Arctic and Antarctic. They also use icebreakers in the Great Lakes. These vessels make a path in the ice. This helps other vessels pass through. Motor lifeboats (MLBs) are another type of USCG vessel. Guardsmen use these boats to rescue people. MLBs can handle rough seas. If an MLB tips over, it can right itself in thirty seconds.

ASTs go through cliff rescue training and other types of scenarios to make sure they are prepared.

Another important job is an aviation survival technician (AST). ASTs are rescue swimmers. Their job is dangerous. It requires intense training. During emergencies, ASTs are in the middle of the action. Sometimes boats overturn in bad weather. ASTs rescue people from rough seas. They can also rescue people stranded on cliffs. They dangle from helicopters to rescue people this way.

ASTs provide lifesaving treatment. They are also technicians. They know how to maintain aircraft equipment. Petty Officer Kyle Stallings is an AST. He says, "Nothing is going to be harder than what they train us for. And you're always ready, you never know what you're [going to] get."[3]

SUPPORT JOBS

Some Guardsmen have support jobs. They assist other Guardsmen and

The USCG uses booms to contain oil spills. Booms are floating barriers.

USCG operations. One support job is a culinary specialist (CS). A CS creates and cooks nutritious meals. Ava Frickey is a CS. She prepares food for more than one hundred Guardsmen aboard a cutter. She describes her job as "a balancing act." She says, "That's especially true when you're at sea with 15-foot [5-m] waves."[4] She handles knives and other tools while on a moving boat.

Other support jobs include health services technician (HS), marine science technician (MST), and yeoman. HSs treat sick or injured Guardsmen. They assist doctors and dentists. They can give medication. They can also handle medical emergencies.

An MST's goal is to protect the marine environment. MSTs supervise the cleanup after an oil spill. They also patrol harbors. They do vessel safety checks too.

Yeomen work in offices. Most are stationed on land. They are organized. They have computer and people skills. They help other Guardsmen with their career choices. They share information about educational and training programs. They answer questions and give advice.

OFFICER CAREERS

Some Guardsmen advance to become officers. Officers are leaders. They manage other Guardsmen. They plan missions and give orders. There are several ways to become an officer. One option is to enroll in the Coast Guard Academy after high school. This academy is a military college. It is in New London, Connecticut. Students are called cadets. Most cadets study engineering and computer science. They also study environmental science. Cadets train to be officers. After four years, they graduate with a college degree.

WOMEN IN THE COAST GUARD

Before 1975, women were not allowed to attend the Coast Guard Academy. Even after women were accepted, they had fewer opportunities than men. They could not serve on cutters. They were not allowed to do some jobs. That changed in 1978. In that year, the USCG opened all officer and enlisted jobs to women.

They are known as ensigns. An ensign is the lowest-ranking officer.

Another option for people who want to become officers is Officer Candidate School. This is a seventeen-week course. It is held in Yorktown, Virginia. It is for college graduates. They may be **civilians** or enlisted members of the USCG. Graduates of the program become ensigns.

College students can become officers through the College Student Pre-Commissioning Initiative (CSPI). This program is open to students in their second year of college. The CSPI helps pay a

Students go through a special ceremony after they graduate from Officer Candidate School.

student's college costs. Students complete their degree as well as basic training and officer training.

CHAPTER THREE

WHAT IS A TYPICAL DAY LIKE IN THE COAST GUARD?

Guardsmen serve around the world. But most are stationed along US coasts. Others patrol inland waterways such as lakes. USCG centers on land are called shore stations. Guardsmen launch vessels from these stations. Other USCG

Guardsmen at air stations are prepared to respond to emergencies. There are twenty-four USCG air stations in the United States.

locations are air stations. Aircraft crews are based at these stations.

Many Guardsmen live and work on cutters. The USCG **deploys** some Guardsmen. They leave their station. They may spend weeks or months away

Boatswain's mates can navigate lifeboats. They use radio communication to talk to other Guardsmen.

from home. Deployment usually lasts less than a year.

Guardsmen are ready to tackle challenging tasks. Each day, the USCG responds to about forty-five SAR cases.

It boards about 140 vessels. It responds to twenty oil or chemical spills.

HOUSING

Guardsmen receive help finding housing. Housing may be on the station where they are based. The housing differs from station to station. Newly enlisted Guardsmen who are single usually live in barracks. A barrack is a large building with many rooms. Guardsmen may share rooms. They sleep on bunk beds. Married Guardsmen have on- and off-base housing choices. Some live in apartments. Others live in townhouses or single-family homes.

CONTINUING EDUCATION

Guardsmen can go to specialized training centers. These are called "A" schools. They are located across the country. Some qualified Guardsmen go directly to "A" school after basic training. But most first spend at least a few months at their assignment. They can attend "A" school after they choose a job. There are "A" school programs for almost every job.

At an "A" school, Guardsmen learn skills to do a specific job. For example, Guardsmen who want to become EMs go through a nineteen-week program.

ASTs go to an "A" school in North Carolina. They practice swimming while carrying 10-pound (5-kg) weights.

The program is held at the EM "A" school in Yorktown, Virginia.

A DAY IN THE LIFE OF AN AMT

A Guardsman's daily duties depend on his or her job. Petty Officer 2nd Class Miguel Arellano is an AMT. He went to an "A" school for his training. He spends most of his day in aircraft hangars. Aircraft hangars are large buildings. They are used to store planes and other aircraft. Arellano's job includes changing tires, fixing wings, and painting aircraft. But his role changes

THE 9/11 EVACUATION

On September 11, 2001, **terrorists** hijacked four planes. They crashed two planes into the World Trade Center. This building was in Manhattan, New York City. Another plane hit the Pentagon building near Washington, DC. The fourth plane crashed into a field in Pennsylvania. Nearly 3,000 people were killed. Thousands of people ran to the harbor in Manhattan. Twelve USCG patrol boats arrived at the scene. Ferries and other boats also helped. They evacuated more than 500,000 people.

when the SAR alarm goes off. He climbs aboard a helicopter or plane. He becomes part of the flight crew. He operates the hoist. The hoist is a device. It lowers a basket into the water. Survivors climb into the basket. Arellano raises the basket to bring survivors into the aircraft.

Arellano knows his job is important. He says, "When you . . . rescue three people off a sinking ship, that's the true reward. We made it possible to save those lives."[5]

TRACKING ICEBERGS

Guardsmen do many important jobs. Petty Officer 3rd Class Jennifer Crocker is an MST. She is part of the USCG International Ice Patrol. She flies a plane over the North Atlantic Ocean. She looks for icebergs. Icebergs are large, floating pieces of ice. Ships could run into them. This could damage or sink the ships.

Crocker enters information about the icebergs she sees into a computer. The computer uses a program called BergTracker. BergTracker records the iceberg's location, size, and shape. The USCG notes wind conditions and ocean currents. It can predict how the iceberg will drift.

Guardsmen go through water survival training when they need to learn how to use new equipment. They practice wearing and using this equipment in the water.

LIFE AT SEA

Other Guardsmen spend entire days at sea. Lieutenant Commander Charlene Criss is a physician's assistant (PA). She treats people who get sick or injured. She works and lives aboard the *Eagle*. Coast Guard Academy cadets train on this ship. They spend up to six weeks at sea. Criss spends part of her day in the *Eagle*'s sick bay. Cadets go to the sick bay when they feel unwell. Then Criss treats them.

Criss hands out seasickness pills and patches. She makes sure the crew does not get dehydrated or sunburned. Sometimes PAs have to deal with serious illnesses and injuries. Once, Criss treated the entire crew for food poisoning.

Working on a ship can be dangerous. Heavy equipment can fall and hurt the crew.

CANINE COASTIES

Trained dogs serve alongside Guardsmen. Some are trained to detect explosives. They work at **ports** and in warehouses. They also work on vessels. They can sniff out bombs and illegal cargo. Guardsmen may bring the dogs on aircraft to reach vessels at sea. Guardsmen lift and lower the dogs from the aircraft. The dogs wear eye goggles and ear protection. The gear protects them from sea spray, flying debris, and loud engine noises.

PAs do the best they can with the limited supplies that can fit on board. Criss says, "There's pressure because you have to make a lot of decisions. A lot of times, you're on your own and have to rely on your own knowledge and skills."[6]

CHAPTER FOUR

WHERE DO GUARDSMEN SERVE?

USCG stations in the United States are located in two areas. These areas are called the Atlantic and Pacific commands. The Pacific command is made up of four districts. There are five districts in the Atlantic command. Districts are divided into smaller areas. These areas

Some Guardsmen work and train in other countries such as South Korea.

are called sectors. Each sector contains stations. Guardsmen stay at their station for two to four years. Then they are reassigned. They move to another station.

AIR STATION CAPE COD

The USCG Air Station Cape Cod (ASCC) is in Massachusetts. It is the only USCG air station in the northeast. Pilots respond to emergency calls. They launch aircraft within thirty minutes of receiving a call. They patrol the waters from New Jersey up to the Canadian border.

Guardsmen at the ASCC carry out many tasks. They conduct SAR missions off the coast. They work with other stations, vessels, and aircraft. Teamwork helps ensure the success of a mission.

In 2016, Petty Officer 3rd Class Evan Staph and Lieutenant John Hess were working at the ASCC. Staph is a rescue swimmer. Hess is a helicopter pilot.

This map shows the states that are in the Atlantic and Pacific commands.

They responded to an emergency call.

They rescued two sailors caught in a storm off the coast. There were 40-foot (12-m) waves and strong winds. One of the hoists broke during the rescue. It would not pull up fast enough. Staph and Hess worked together. They were able to pull the sailors into the helicopter. Hess said, "It was an all hands on deck effort. Everyone was at work that day doing their part."[7] Hess and Staph received awards for the success of this mission. They were awarded for their heroism.

Guardsmen at the ASCC also patrol fishing areas. They enforce fishing laws. They help clean up oil and chemical spills. From the air, Guardsmen protect local ports. They watch for illegal activity such as drug smuggling.

Guardsmen from the ASCC practice lowering a rescue basket on an island in the Gulf of Maine.

THE SAGINAW RIVER STATION

Other USCG stations are in or near inland waterways. One such station is on the Saginaw River in Essexville, Michigan. Guardsmen at this station patrol

Saginaw Bay and the Saginaw River. Their **fleet** is made up of three boats.

The Saginaw River station is especially busy in winter. Ice fishing and snow sports are popular. People often venture out onto the frozen Saginaw Bay. Some ice may not be thick enough to hold a person's weight. Guardsmen are always ready to rescue people. On one day in March 2019, five people needed rescuing within an hour. All of them were stranded on ice floes in the river. Ice floes are floating ice patches. Guardsmen rescued two of these people. Civilians helped rescue the other three.

Guardsmen practice ice rescue drills on the Saginaw River.

PATROLLING THE PACIFIC

District Fourteen covers 14 million square miles (36 million sq km) of land and water in the Pacific Ocean. The Coast Guard has stations on the Hawaiian Islands. USCG Base Honolulu is on Sand Island. This island is off the coast of Honolulu, Hawaii. Guardsmen at this station have many jobs. They enforce maritime laws and keep ports safe. They search for illegal drugs. They keep people from entering the country illegally. They also maintain navigation equipment such as beacons. Beacons are lights that act as signals or warnings.

Guardsmen at this base also protect the environment. In November 2019, a ship spilled oil into the North Pacific Ocean. The USCG flew a helicopter over the area.

Coast Guard cutters patrol around the island of Oahu in Hawaii.

The Guardsmen saw oil spreading toward Sand Island. Two USCG vessels placed a barrier in the water. The barrier stopped the oil from spreading.

Guardsmen at Base Honolulu may be assigned special missions. Hawaii is home to the active volcano Kilauea. Hot lava flows into the ocean when the volcano erupts.

The lava makes the water scalding hot. It causes steam explosions. Active volcanoes also produce dangerous gases. Guardsmen must protect people from these dangers. They set up a safety zone where the lava flows. People must stay outside the zone.

DEEPWATER HORIZON

On April 20, 2010, an oil rig in the Gulf of Mexico exploded. Oil rigs drill for oil under the seafloor. The rig was called Deepwater Horizon. Eleven people died in the explosion. USCG aircraft responded. Guardsmen rescued 115 workers. Millions of gallons of oil spilled into the water. The cleanup process took a few months. Thousands of Guardsmen helped with this effort. They set up barriers to stop the oil from spreading.

DEPLOYED AT SEA

Some Guardsmen are deployed on cutters. One USCG cutter is called the *Healy*. Its home base is Seattle, Washington. It is an icebreaker ship. This type of ship is powerful enough to break through ice. Each year in the summer, the *Healy* makes several trips to the Arctic. Some of its trips have lasted up to six months.

The *Healy* is also a research ship. Its crew is made up of Guardsmen and scientists. Scientists conduct many experiments in the Arctic. They gather information about ocean currents, wildlife, and water quality. Guardsmen on the *Healy* work to protect the environment. They help enforce laws in the Arctic. They also perform SAR missions when needed.

Ced The first thing Guardsmen on an icebreaker must get used to is the noise. The ship makes a lot of noise as it breaks through ice. This action also makes the ship shake.

Room on board an icebreaker may be tight. Crew members often share sleeping rooms. In each room is a bathroom and three to six bunk beds.

There are several rules *Healy* crew members need to follow. Many of these rules are for safety. Each person logs in for attendance twice a day. The captain checks to make sure everyone is on board. There are also many emergency drills. The crew practices what to do if there is a fire.

RESCUING SHIPS

In 2012, a tanker ship was stuck in the ice during a bad storm in the Arctic. It was delivering fuel to Nome, Alaska. The crew of the *Healy* came to the rescue. The *Healy* cleared a path for the tanker. It broke through 300 miles (480 km) of ice. With the help of the USCG, the tanker reached Nome.

Everyone must know how to abandon ship in an emergency.

Some crew members are seamen. They keep the ship working. They repair SAR gear and small boats. They use cranes to lift and lower equipment. On the *Healy*, seamen also work with sea charts and plot routes.

Deirdre Gray is a seaman on the *Healy*. She says that the work can be tiring. Crew members start their days at 8:00 a.m. They may not finish their work until 10:00 p.m. But Gray finds her job rewarding. She explains, "These are things that, outside of

The **Healy** *is the Coast Guard's largest icebreaker.*

the military, I don't think I would have ever had the experience to see or do."[8]

 Guardsmen work around the clock every day. They ensure the safety of the country's coastlines and waterways. They are always ready to respond to a crisis. Guardsmen take risks every day. They put their lives on the line. Their teamwork helps keep Americans safe.

GLOSSARY

aptitude

a person's ability to do or learn something

civilians

people who are not in the military

deploys

sends a person or a military unit to another location

enlistment

the process of joining the armed services

fleet

a group of ships that are under the command of one officer

maritime

having to do with the sea

ports

towns or cities that have a harbor where ships are kept

terrorists

people who attack or threaten others

vessel

any type of watercraft that can be used for transportation

SOURCE NOTES

CHAPTER ONE: HOW DO PEOPLE JOIN THE COAST GUARD?

1. Quoted in Karen Knight, "Coast Guard Recruiters Remain Vital," *Cape May County Herald*, May 29, 2019. www.capemaycountyherald.com.

2. Quoted in Marisa Iati, "A Rare, Behind-the-Scenes Look at Coast Guard Training in Cape May," *NJ.com*, September 24, 2017. www.nj.com.

CHAPTER TWO: WHAT JOBS DOES THE COAST GUARD OFFER?

3. Quoted in Kristina Yates, "I Get Paid to Be a Rescue Swimmer," *CNBC*, May 18, 2016. www.cnbc.com.

4. Quoted in "A Coast Guard Life – Ava Frickey," *YouTube*, April 11, 2017. www.youtube.com.

CHAPTER THREE: WHAT IS A TYPICAL DAY LIKE IN THE COAST GUARD?

5. Quoted in LT Stephanie Young, "Keeping the Coast Guard Airborne," *Coast Guard Compass*, February 2, 2012. https://coastguard.dodlive.mil.

6. Quoted in Hillel Kutler, "U.S. Coast Guard PAs Aboard the *Eagle*," *American Academy of Physician Assistants*, November 2016. www.aapa.org.

CHAPTER FOUR: WHERE DO GUARDSMEN SERVE?

7. Quoted in Diana Sherbs, "Honor, Respect, Devotion to Duty: CGNR 6033 Crew, Air Station Cape Cod," *Coast Guard Compass*, September 25, 2015. https://coastguard.dodlive.mil.

8. Quoted in "Coast Guard Reserve," *Today's Military*, 2020. www.todaysmilitary.com.

FOR FURTHER RESEARCH

BOOKS

Roberta Baxter, *Work in the Military*. San Diego, CA: ReferencePoint Press, 2020.

Barbara M. Linde, *Military Courts*. New York: PowerKids Press, 2019.

Brett S. Martin, *Military Robots*. Minneapolis, MN: Abdo Publishing 2019.

Vince Toth, *My Sister Is in the Coast Guard*. New York: PowerKids Press, 2016.

INTERNET SOURCES

"A Day in the Life of a Helicopter Rescue," *GoCoastGuard.com*, 2019. www.gocoastguard.com.

"Active-Duty Careers," *GoCoastGuard.com*, 2019. www.gocoastguard.com.

Meredith Manning, "Kids Don't Float Teaches Children Lessons for Life," *Coast Guard Alaska*, March 7, 2016. alaska.coastguard.dodlive.mil.

"Officer Candidate School (OCS)," *GoCoastGuard.com*, 2019. www.gocoastguard.com.

WEBSITES

Today's Military
www.todaysmilitary.com

This site gives helpful information about the different branches of the US military. Visitors to the site can learn about USCG careers, training, and many other topics.

US Coast Guard
www.gocoastguard.com

The USCG's website has information about requirements, basic training, and jobs in the Coast Guard. It also shares information about missions and life in the Coast Guard.

US Department of Homeland Security: Coast Guard
www.uscg.mil

The US Department of Homeland Security's Coast Guard website educates people about the USCG. The site shares important information, including news and the history of the USCG.

INDEX

"A" school, 5, 50–52
Air Station Cape Cod (ASCC), 59–62
Armed Services Vocational Aptitude Battery (ASVAB) test, 16–18
aviation maintenance technicians (AMTs), 37, 51–53
aviation survival technicians (ASTs), 38–39
avionics electrical technicians (AETs), 36–37

Base Honolulu, 66–67
boatswain's mates (BMs), 30–31
boot camp, 18–27

Coast Guard Academy, 42–43, 56
College Student Pre-Commissioning Initiative (CSPI), 44–45
culinary specialists (CSs), 40–41
cutters, 5, 30, 40, 43, 47, 69–72

damage controlmen (DCs), 33–34

electrician's mates (EMs), 34–35, 50
electronics technicians, 35
enlisting, 16–27

Golden Ray, 6–9
gunner's mates (GMs), 31–32

health services technicians (HSs), 41
Healy, 69–72
housing, 49

icebreakers, 37, 69–72

marine science technicians (MSTs), 41, 54
Maritime Enforcement Specialists (MEs), 32

Officer Candidate School, 44
oil spills, 4, 41, 49, 62, 66–67, 68

recruiters, 15

Saginaw River station, 63–64
search-and-rescue (SAR) missions, 28, 31, 36, 48, 53, 60, 70, 72

US Coast Guard Reserve, 4, 18, 26

yeomen, 42

IMAGE CREDITS

Cover: PA3 Barbara L. Patton/U.S. Coast Guard/DVIDS
5: Petty Officer 1st Class Bradley Pigage/US Coast Guard/DVIDS
7: Petty Officer 3rd Class Paige Hause/US Coast Guard/DVIDS
8: Petty Officer 3rd Class Ryan Dickinson/US Coast Guard/DVIDS
11: © cpaulfell/Shutterstock Images
13: © Jerry Zitterman/Shutterstock Images
17: Spc. Andrew Ingram/DVIDS
19: Chief Warrant Officer John Edwards/US Coast Guard/DVIDS
22: Chief Warrant Officer Donnie Brzuska/US Coast Guard/DVIDS
25: Seaman Josalyn Brown/US Coast Guard/DVIDS
29: Petty Officer 1st Class John Luck/US Coast Guard/DVIDS
31: © Leonard Zhukovsky/Shutterstock Images
33: Petty Officer 2nd Class Michael De Nyse/US Coast Guard/DVIDS
34: Petty Officer 2nd Class Annie R. B. Elis/US Coast Guard/DVIDS
38: Petty Officer 2nd Class Jordan Akiyama/US Coast Guard/DVIDS
40: Petty Officer 2nd Class Ryan Tippets/US Coast Guard/DVIDS
45: Petty Officer 3rd Class Diana Sherbs/US Coast Guard/DVIDS
47: US Coast Guard/DVIDS
48: Petty Officer 1st Class Levi Read/US Coast Guard/DVIDS
51: Seaman Ryan Fisher/US Coast Guard/DVIDS
55: Petty Officer 1st Class Matthew S. Masaschi/US Coast Guard/DVIDS
59: Petty Officer 1st Class Matthew S. Masaschi/US Coast Guard/DVIDS
61: © Red Line Editorial
63: Petty Officer 1st Class Justin Munk/US Coast Guard/DVIDS
65: Chief Petty Officer John Masson/US Coast Guard/DVIDS
67: Petty Officer 3rd Class Matthew West/US Coast Guard/DVIDS
73: Senior Chief Petty Officer NyxoLyno Cangemi/US Coast Guard/DVIDS

ABOUT THE AUTHOR

Cecilia Pinto McCarthy has written more than thirty-five nonfiction books for young readers. When she is not writing, she teaches ecology classes at a nature sanctuary. She lives north of Boston, Massachusetts, with her family.